Tikki Turtle's Quest

Written & Illustrated
by Gill McBarnet

Dedicated to **my** young ones ~ Eddie, Will and Tara

One day, Tikki Turtle was ready to lay her eggs, so away she went to search for the perfect place. Where would the perfect place be?

Would it be out in the deep blue sea where baby dolphin is born? "This is perfect…" said Mother Dolphin, as she nursed her newborn baby.

Mother Whale also had her baby in the deep blue sea...

...and so did Mother Eagle Ray.

"Too deep!" said Tikki to her friends the dolphin, whale and eagle ray. "What if my eggs drop down, down, down to the bottom of the sea?"

"Good for you but not for me
so I'll continue to search the sea."

And she swam closer to shore where it was not so deep.

Some jellyfish drifted by.

Mother Jellyfish was holding her eggs in her frilly arms, as she drifted peacefully along.

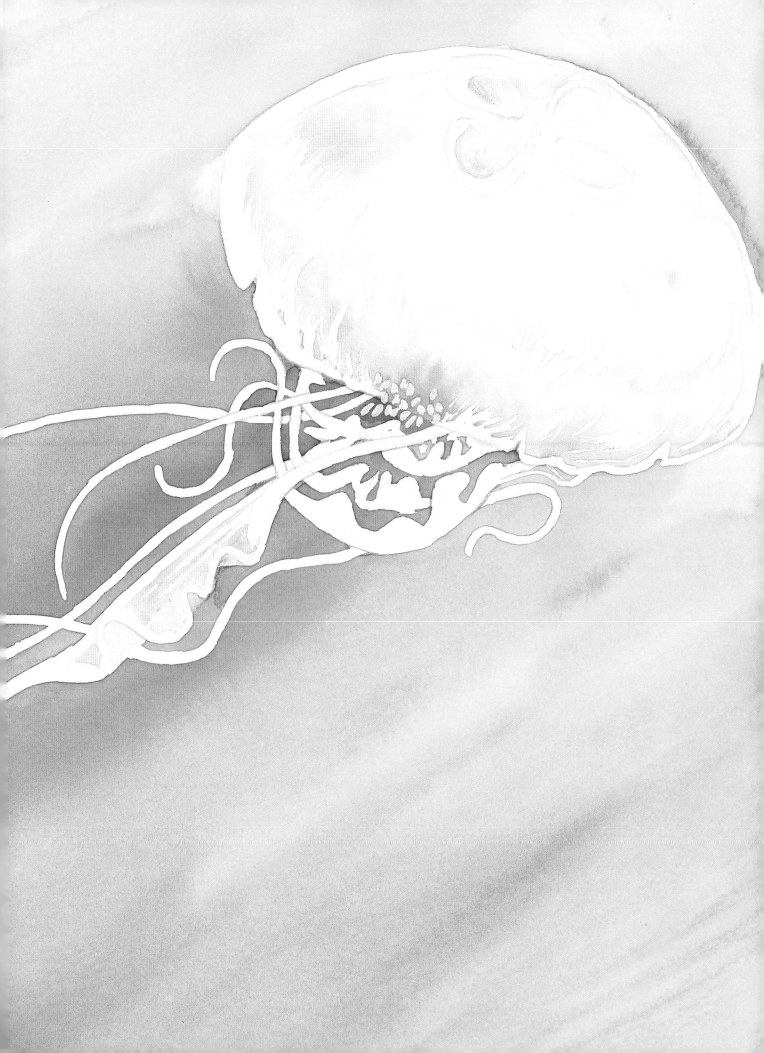

Father Seahorse had a pouch full of eggs which had been laid there by Mother Seahorse...

...while Father Cardinal fish kept his eggs in his mouth!

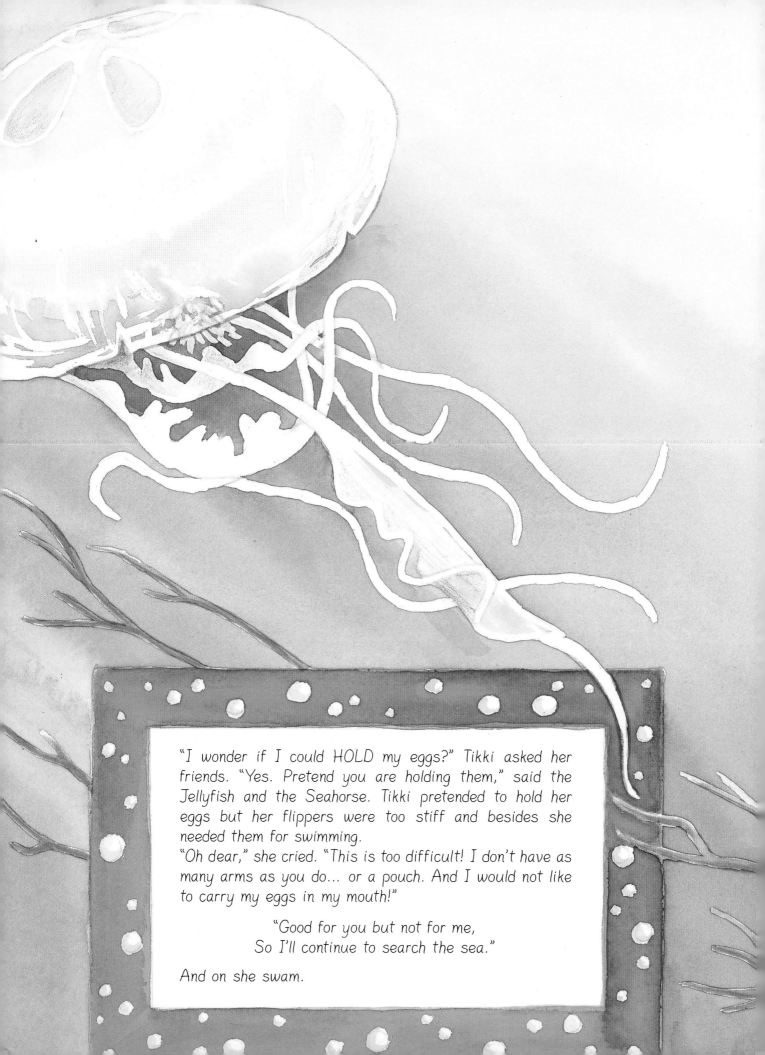

"I wonder if I could HOLD my eggs?" Tikki asked her friends. "Yes. Pretend you are holding them," said the Jellyfish and the Seahorse. Tikki pretended to hold her eggs but her flippers were too stiff and besides she needed them for swimming.

"Oh dear," she cried. "This is too difficult! I don't have as many arms as you do... or a pouch. And I would not like to carry my eggs in my mouth!"

"Good for you but not for me,
So I'll continue to search the sea."

And on she swam.

Tikki Turtle swam closer to the shore, to the coral reef. Under a rocky ledge was a cave, where Mother Octopus had laid her eggs. Her eggs were hanging like clusters of pearls and Mother Octopus was guarding them until they were ready to hatch.

"Find a cave as I have done," suggested Mother Octopus, helpfully. "It's quite a tight squeeze for me, but perfect for my eggs."

"You're very kind," Tikki replied, "...but no thank you. I cannot hang my eggs in clusters and besides, a cave would feel too tight for me."

"Good for you but not for me,
So I'll continue to search the sea."

And on she swam.

Tikki Turtle explored the reef.

It was warm and pleasant with plenty of seaweed for a turtle to munch, but it was also very BUSY. There were big fish and little fish everywhere, in many different shapes and colors.

"Join us here. It's a perfect place for eggs!" the fish exclaimed, happily. "We simply scatter our eggs, and they drift about in the water until the little ones are ready to hatch..."

Sure enough, the water was speckled with their eggs. "TOO BUSY!" said Tikki Turtle. "I couldn't bear to think of my eggs in such a busy place, and I would not want to scatter them all about!"

"Good for you but not for me,
So I'll continue to search the sea."

And on she swam, even closer to shore.

Tikki came to where the anemones and coral were clustered like flowers on the rocks.
"Our eggs become baby buds, and they join us on the rocks..." said the anemones and the coral. "Care to join us?" they enquired.

"Too bumpy and scratchy," Tikki replied.

"Good for you but not for me,
and now I'm tired as tired can be.
I'm tired of searching and searching the sea!"

And on she wearily went to a tide pool, where she stopped to look at her reflection. It was tiring, searching for the perfect place …and she had to find a place SOON, because her eggs were ready to be laid.

In the pool, Tikki saw some crabs and shrimp. They had their eggs safely tucked beneath their bodies. "This tide pool seems peaceful. Perhaps I can lay my eggs here…" Tikki said to the crabs and shrimp. But before they could reply…

...CRASH!

A giant wave smashed against the rocks. Tikki turned and saw another wave about to crash into the pool.

"TOO NOISY!" shouted Tikki above the crashing waves, and she quickly swam away.

The sun was setting as she limped slowly up onto the beach.
"Oh dear," she cried. "I've searched and searched for the perfect place to lay my eggs, but all that I can find is too deep, too difficult, too tight, too busy, too scattered, too bumpy or too noisy. Good for my friends, but not for me."
Sadly, Tikki rested her head on the soft sand.
"Wait a minute!" she exclaimed, looking down at the sand.
"The sand feels good. What about the BEACH for my eggs?"

Mother Monk Seal smiled and said,

"What's good for you is good for me.
As you can very clearly see...
Dry land is where we need to be!"

That night when the moon was bright, Tikki dug a hole in the sand. It was not too deep, too difficult, too tight, too scattered, too busy, too bumpy or too noisy. "Ah!" she sighed. "My nest in the sand is soft and warm and just right for my eggs." Tikki Turtle's quest was over. She had found the perfect place to lay her eggs.

"Mahalo" to Jayme Perrello of the Maui Ocean Center,
and family & friends who encouraged "Tikki Turtle's Quest".

Other Titles by Gill McBarnet:
The Gift of Aloha
Gecko Hide and Seek
The Goodnight Gecko
The Shark Who Learned a Lesson
The Whale Who Wanted to be Small
The Wonderful Journey
A Whale's Tale
The Brave Little Turtle

First published 2000 by Ruwanga Trading
ISBN 0-9701528-0-9

Printed in the People's Republic of China through Everbest Printers

BOOK ENQUIRIES:
Booklines Hawaii Ltd.,
94-527 Puahi Street,
Waipahu, HI 96797
Email: bookline@lava.net